Frankie on the Run

This Book
belongs to
~~Brit~~ Brittany
Bracken!! !! !! !!
☺ ☺ ☺ ☺

For my daughter Brenna,
who shares my love of pigs and words.

© 1995 Linda Holeman (text)
© 1995 Heather Collins (illustration)

Boardwalk Books

Canadian Catalogue in Publication Data

Holeman, Linda, 1949–
    Frankie on the run

ISBN 1–895681–09–X

I. Title

PS8565.O622F7 1995   jC813'.54   C95–931664–7
PZ7.H65Fr 1995

Design, Electronic Composition, and Production
by Blair Kerrigan/Glyphics

Printed and bound in Canada
by Webcom

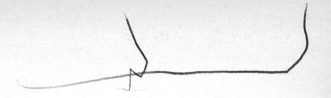

LINDA HOLEMAN

Frankie on the Run

ILLUSTRATIONS BY HEATHER COLLINS

Boardwalk Books

CHAPTER 1

Frankie wiggled his round behind. He shuffled his feet on the rough floor. He stretched his short neck.

Frankie was not comfortable. And he was a little worried.

He didn't like being crowded into the back of Farmer Halley's truck. The jangling milk cans were noisy. The bales of prickly straw made him sneeze. The truck bounced and jiggled on the hard dirt road, and Frankie thought about home. He wanted to have his gentle morning root in the trough, looking for Ma Halley's breakfast flapjacks. He wanted to roll in the soft, sweet dust under the warm afternoon sun. He wanted to lie quietly, listening to slow evening raindrops bounce off the leaves of the nannyberry bush that hung over the pigpen fence.

His eyelids started to close, as he thought about his favourite country pig things. But the noise and the tickling in his nostrils and the loose board banging against his ear each time the truck hit a bump kept him awake.

Finally the truck stopped. The back opened, and Farmer Halley called Frankie. "Pig, pig, pig . . . come on, Frankie." He was smiling at Frankie.

Frankie trotted along the board Farmer Halley had put down, and followed the tall, thin man into a low, square building.

Maybe it's another contest, Frankie thought, looking around for the other pigs. He had so enjoyed himself at the Fair last year.

Farmer Halley led him to a pen, and Frankie scampered in. The farmer closed the gate with a bang.

"So long, Frankie," he said and, putting his hands in his pockets, walked away whistling.

Frankie lifted his snout in a farewell salute. He looked into the next pen and saw a huge, black hog lying on his side.

"Hello, there," Frankie said politely.

The hog raised his head. His broad snout was covered in coarse bristles.

He stared at Frankie, and his small eyes narrowed. Then he let his big head flop back to the ground.

Frankie ignored the hog's poor manners. "When does the judging begin?" he asked, still keeping his voice pleasant.

The hog didn't even bother to raise his head this time.

"What judging?" he grumbled.

"The contests, of course," Frankie said. "I won a blue ribbon for silkiest skin last year. Ma Halley had just given me a good scrub, and my skin does glow wonderfully after a scrub." He realized his neighbour might think he was bragging. "But of course," he said, "there *were* only two other pigs entered."

The black hog grunted. "This is no contest, bud."

Before Frankie could ask anything else, a man in high rubber boots walked up to the pen next to his. The man threw in a rope, easily looping it around the hog's thick neck. As he opened the gate and gave a hard tug on the rope, the gigantic black hog came to life. He leaped and twisted in the air. His snorts were loud and rude.

"It's the end of the line!" he squealed to Frankie. "Wake up, Pinky! This is where you turn into bacon!"

Frankie stood very still for a moment, watching the struggling hog disappear with the man. It couldn't be. Farmer Halley would never do this. And Ma Halley was always so kind to Frankie, bringing him special treats, and singing as she brushed his skin with a lovely wire brush.

Bacon! Frankie shuddered.

"It must be a mistake," he

whispered. He was sure it was all a mistake. But perhaps he should find out for himself.

He sniffed round and round his pen, nudging and poking at its wooden bars. He pushed hard in one corner where a board felt loose. It hurt his nose, but he grunted and worked until the board made a crunching sound and broke in half. Frankie flopped down on his belly and wriggled through the hole. He crept by the outside of the pen, and then slunk along the wall of the building. Finally he came to a doorway, and peeked in.

A woman in a hair net, wearing a stained, white coat, was holding the lever of a big machine. The machine thumped and whirred, and Frankie's eyes grew round with horror as he saw what was sliding down a narrow chute.

Sausage links!

CHAPTER 2

Frankie shook his head to stop it from spinning. The black hog had been right after all.

Steady now, he told himself. There must be a way out of this mess. He looked beyond the machine to a door at the far end of the room. It was open a tiny crack. He could see blue sky!

Head down, he tiptoed through the sausage–making room, trying not to look at the dreadful chute. The woman was watching the sausages, and the machine was noisy as it clanked out the never–ending chain of fat pork loops.

As he inched along behind the woman, Frankie's breath came in tiny, gasping oinks. He thought he might faint. He wondered if he would make it to the door, or collapse and be discovered.

But his legs kept moving, and suddenly he was outside. He shakily filled his lungs with fresh air and looked around. He was in a big yard surrounded by a low fence. Beyond the fence was a tangle of small trees.

It's my only chance, Frankie thought, biting his bottom lip as he stared at the trees. He put his head down and bravely charged at the fence. When it was only a snout away, he shut his eyes and jumped.

Frankie had never jumped before.

"Whee! Whee!" he squealed, both excited and terrified, as he sailed over the fence. The landing wasn't at all smooth. His bottom still up in the air, he skidded along on the stony ground, giving his chin and his left elbow a nasty scrape.

He knew there was no time to spare. Picking himself up, he raced towards the safety of the woods. Then he burrowed into a mass of high weeds growing under the trees.

He crouched there, trembling. He was achy and scared and alone. He missed his soft bed, his nannyberry bush, and his food trough. It was the first time he had been away from everything he knew.

Farmer Halley couldn't have known what that terrible place really was, Frankie thought. He would never do that to me.

He finally lay on his side so he could see the circle of sky above the slightly moving weeds. The sky grew a lighter blue, then slowly changed to a beautiful rosy colour. When the last streaks of pink had faded, and the sky was turning dark, Frankie's tears started.

. . . . . .

Frankie stretched, then stopped suddenly. The stretching hurt his torn elbow. He opened one eye, then another. Bright sunlight.

It was morning, and Frankie was dreadfully hungry. Being careful of his elbow, he cautiously crawled out of his weedy bed. He sniffed the air. There was a lovely stale odour coming from somewhere. He followed the smell through the trees and across a small field of grass. He came to a wooden picnic table. Beside it sat a big green container. He put his front feet against the hard green plastic, trying to get a better sniff, and the container fell over with a thud.

Frankie dined magnificently on two mouldy doughnuts and a black banana. He finished up with a delightful hamburger wrapper, damp with grease and ketchup.

He felt like a new pig. Now to find his way back to the farm. Farmer Halley would be so pleased to see him.

Wouldn't he?

CHAPTER 3

Frankie walked and walked over the neatly cut grass. He wondered if he was heading in the direction of the farm. Finally he came upon a gravel path. He felt encouraged by the path and trotted along importantly. He liked the feel of his hard feet hitting the thick broken stones. Small, satisfying puffs of dust rose up around his legs.

Following the path through a clump of trees, he saw a wooden bench. Sitting on it was a woman who looked a little like Ma Halley.

But instead of a flowered dress and crisp white apron, she wore a heavy brown coat and a blue wool cap pulled low on her forehead.

"Hello there, stranger," she said. "Are you hungry?" She dug through the plastic bags piled around her on the bench.

"Aha!" she said, and held up half an egg sandwich. She tore it into two pieces. Even though he had just eaten, Frankie could always manage another bite. He graciously accepted the food. While he was busy chewing, the woman gathered up her bags, put them into an old wagon, and walked away. As she walked, she scattered pieces of her sandwich. Pigeons appeared out of nowhere, flying down behind her to peck at the crumbs.

She was nice, Frankie thought, as the woman and her wagon

disappeared. Nice, but no help in getting me home.

He kept on the path, enjoying the warm sun. Every few minutes he would stop to smell the starry, red and white throats of the petunias and the hard, yellow heads of the marigolds planted in flower beds along the way. As he rounded a bend, a man and woman wearing sneakers, shorts, and tie–dyed T–shirts almost ran him over. The woman stopped.

"Look, Chris!" she called after the man. "A pig! What's he doing here?"

The man turned his head but kept running. "Who knows? In this crazy city, anything's possible. Don't lose your pace. Come on, we said we'd beat our best time today."

The woman began jogging on the spot. She took off the band she was wearing around her forehead and slipped it onto Frankie. It fit just below his ears and above his eyes.

"Looking good, piggy," she said, then ran off after the man. Frankie thought about trying to catch up with them, but his tummy was too full to hurry.

The striped band felt warm and snug around his head. He wasn't hungry, and his elbow hardly hurt at all. Frankie strolled along the path, wondering who he would meet next. So far everyone had been very friendly.

After a while he heard voices. He stopped at the sight of bright plastic swings, a high metal slide, and a spinning roundabout.

"Hey! Look over there," a boy with a blue baseball cap shouted to four other children. "It's a pig!"

Frankie slowly backed up as the three boys and two girls ran towards him. They were all yelling at once, and one of the girls twirled a plastic rope with two handles over her head. He thought of the man with the rope, and the way he had slipped it over the black hog's neck.

What were these children going to do to him?

Frankie put on an affectionate expression, but his heart thudded painfully. The children from other farms who came to visit the Halleys had been gentle with Frankie, patting him and feeding him treats.

But these children seemed louder and rougher, pushing each other as they scrambled toward him.

"He's *so* cute!" one girl said, bending down until her braids tickled Frankie's nose.

"I'm going to ride him," a boy wearing a cowboy hat said, trying to throw his leg over Frankie's broad back. Frankie stepped aside quickly, fixing a stern eye on the boy.

"Let's take him home!" the smallest girl yelled, jumping up and down. "We can use my skipping rope for a leash!"

"Leave him alone," the girl with the braids said. "Maybe he's scared. Are you scared, pig?"

"He's mine! I saw him first!" the boy in the baseball cap shouted at her, pulling on her arm.

Frankie backed away from the noise. With a tiny hop, he scampered towards the roundabout and put his front feet on the metal edge. Then, his hind legs scrambling, he hoisted up his plump rear end. He turned to face the children.

"Look! He wants a ride," the tallest boy said, and all five of them ran to the carousel. The four oldest grabbed the metal bars on the edges.

"Hang on, Mr. Pig!" the small girl shouted as the others began running, pulling, and then leaping onto the roundabout.

The new twirling sensation delighted Frankie, as the trees and the faces of the children flew by in a whirl of colour. "It's almost like flying!" he squealed.

But as the carousel spun faster and faster, Frankie's feet slipped and slid back and forth on the smooth metal floor. He was thrown from side to side. The head band flew up and away. A curious, unpleasant feeling started in the bottom of his stomach.

As the world whizzed past, all he could think about was the greasy

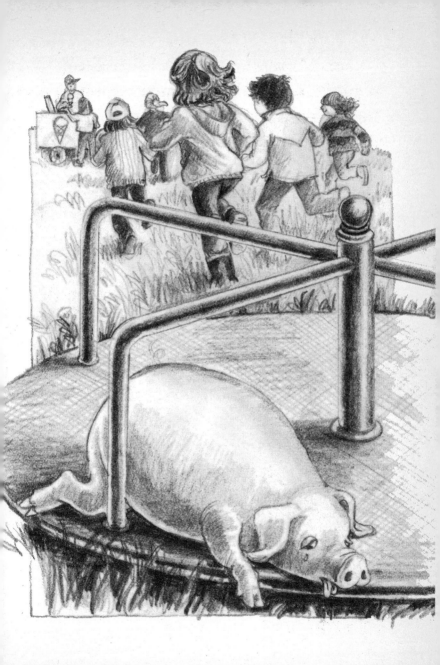

hamburger wrapper and the stale egg sandwich he had eaten earlier. His stomach churned and rolled with the whirling of the roundabout. The children's excited screams hurt his head. Frankie swallowed and swallowed, trying to calm his stomach.

Finally he couldn't stand it any longer. Falling heavily to the floor, he covered his eyes with his front feet.

"Stop! Please stop," he whimpered.

"There's the ice cream man!" one of the children yelled. The carousel jerked, and Frankie uncovered his eyes enough to see the children jumping off. They all ran after a man slowly pedalling down the park path on his ice cream bicycle.

The carousel's spinning grew slower and slower. Then it stopped. Frankie lay still, blinking his eyes. He listened to the faint tinkle of the ice cream bell, and the high voices of the children in the distance.

Frankie wanted to get off the carousel before the children decided to come back. He got to his feet and stepped to the ground. His legs quivered like rubbery pudding. He wobbled away from the carousel and pulled out a mouthful of long green grass. Chewing slowly, he waited for his stomach to settle.

When his legs had stopped shaking and he didn't feel sick any more, Frankie crept into a grove of trees on the other side of the playground. He found a shady hollow beneath a group of tall poplar trees, and lay down. He listened to the rustling lullaby of the broad, shiny leaves.

Exhausted after the dreadful carousel ride, no morning nap, and all the walking, Frankie quickly fell into a deep sleep.

He slept and slept.

. . . . . .

When Frankie awoke, the shadows were long. He lay there, thinking about Farmer Halley. About the smile on Farmer Halley's face as he had unloaded him off the truck.

Frankie got to his feet. Perhaps it wasn't a mistake, he thought to himself, giving his back a good scratch on the rough bark of the closest poplar tree. Perhaps Farmer Halley did intend to leave me at that horrible place. Maybe the smile had, after all, been a rather sly one.

Frankie stopped scratching and looked around. If he couldn't go home, where would he go, and what would he do?

He thought for a minute. His stomach rumbled. He was hungry again, and before too long it would be dark.

The thought of another lonely night was too much for Frankie.

"What's to become of me?" he wailed, throwing his head back. "I've no home and no one to love me. Oh dear, oh dear!" His sobs grew louder and louder.

"Cool it, bro," a voice suddenly hissed from above.

Frankie closed his mouth. He hiccuped, then slowly put his head back even further, so his moist nose was pointing skyward. A pair of mean green eyes stared down at him through the leaves.

CHAPTER 5

The raspy voice spoke again. "You just scared away my dinner. I was all ready to pounce on a juicy meal when you started your crybaby act."

"I'm *so* sorry," Frankie apologized, watching the orange and white striped cat step through the branches hanging over the pathway. He noticed the cat had only one ear. "It's just that I'm not used to being on my own.

There's no one to bring me my meals, or throw a forkful of fresh straw down for me to sleep on. Or scratch behind my ears."

"Well, boo—hoo," the cat answered, without any sympathy at all. "Welcome to the real world, my friend. I've been on my own my whole life, and you don't hear me howling."

Frankie looked at the striped cat with new respect. "Your whole life? My, you must be very brave. And ever so clever. Perhaps you could teach me a few tricks. Sir."

The cat looked down at Frankie's round, hopeful face, then at his chubby, pink body.

"Don't think so. Nope. You just haven't got what it takes for the wild life, pal. You wouldn't last a week out here, with the dogs and kids and park patrols."

Frankie sat down. "But I've nowhere to go," he said quietly, with as much dignity as he could manage. "Do you know any place where a fellow could bed down for the night?"

The cat's scarred face stared into Frankie's. "Well, a few of us have claimed a spot under the walking bridge. About a kilometre from here. No one usually bothers us. If it's okay with the Boss, you can spend the night there. But just one night," he added quickly, seeing the relief on Frankie's face. "The other guys don't like strangers."

"I understand perfectly, sir, and I promise I'll move on first thing in the morning. Once I've had a good sleep I'll be able to think about my situation more clearly."

The cat leaped from the branch and landed soundlessly on the soft moss beside Frankie. "Follow me," he said, "but no noise."

Frankie nodded solemnly, and tried to creep through the bushes like the cat. But he made a great racket as he stepped heavily on dry branches and dead leaves, and once he cried out as the sharp twig of a cranberry bush poked him in the eye.

By the time they arrived at the bridge that ran over a shallow stream, Frankie was pooped.

"Stay here," the cat instructed him, "and I'll check with the Boss."

Frankie took a long, wet slurp of the stream, then sat down in the cool mud at the edge of the water.

The orange and white cat was back in less than three minutes. "Bruce says you're in for tonight, as long as you mind your own business," he said. "This way."

Once again, Frankie followed the scrawny cat. He nodded pleasantly as he walked by a group of six other cats who eyed him suspiciously. They all had ears or parts of their tails missing. Their fur was long and rough, with patches torn out in places.

Frankie found himself a dark spot in a far corner under the low wooden bridge. He watched as the cats snarled and snapped at each other over a piece of bagel and a tin can with flecks of tuna still clinging to the sides. When one of them looked over at him, Frankie saw the hungry look in the dark, green eyes. He backed up against the cold stone supports of the bridge, to feel safer.

As darkness swirled around and under the bridge, the cats quieted down. Each made his own circle against an old log or a clump of dead grass, tucked his nose under his paws, and wrapped his tail around himself. Frankie felt his eyelids growing scratchy and heavy. The painful rumbling in his stomach kept him awake for a time, but he eventually fell into an uneasy sleep.

It seemed he had just closed his eyes when a scream brought him to his feet. It was totally black under the bridge. Frankie couldn't see a thing, but a low growling, then a loud hiss and another scream made the soft hairs on the back of his neck stand straight up.

"What is it? What's happening?" he cried into the inky darkness.

A sleek shadow raced by him. "It's the dogs, man. The alley strays from East Sycamore. Run! Run for your life!!"

Frankie had never been afraid of the shaggy, friendly farm dogs, but now all he could make out were glowing red eyes and sharp, gnashing teeth. When he heard excited snuffling coming toward him, Frankie fled from his damp bed beneath the bridge. His small piggy eyes were wide with fear as he tried to see where he was going.

Squealing in terror, he rushed headlong over soggy ground and through scratchy bushes. He fell, over and over, but got up and kept running. Tears streamed down his cheeks. The barking of the dogs and the yowling of the cats grew fainter as he ran farther and farther away in the cool night air.

His short legs ached with the unusual exercise, and just when he felt he couldn't run another step, he smelled a familiar, sweet odour.

He slowed to a trot, his breath coming in quavering gasps. He raised his snout.

The smell was in front of him.

The fresh smell of newly cut grass. He took a cautious step forward, and there was a hollow thud. His foot was on a board. Following his nose, he climbed up a wooden ramp. A final step took him into a load of clean, fragrant grass.

Not caring where he was, Frankie burrowed into the mound with an exhausted sigh.

Tomorrow was time enough to worry about tomorrow. He closed his eyes and let sleep wash over him.

CHAPTER 6

Loud voices and a clanging thump woke Frankie up.

"Close the back gate, Ernie!"

"Got it! Take her away, Lily."

"Thanks. I'll be back for another load in a few hours."

"Okay. The boys will be cutting the south end of the park all morning. I'll make sure they leave it here for you."

There was a low rumbling and vibration underneath Frankie. He shook his head, rubbing at a pesky piece of grass that was stuck up one nostril. He carefully poked his head up through his cool, green covering.

A warm breeze immediately blew back his ears and made his eyes water. He was moving!

He raised his head higher, trying to get his bearings by sniffing, but the air went by too quickly. Looking around, he saw the cab of a truck, and inside, a woman wearing a peaked cap like Farmer Halley's. Then he looked the other way, over the tailgate of the truck, and saw the road winding away behind him. He settled back, knowing the truck was moving too fast for him to jump off.

When the summer sun was directly overhead, warming Frankie's back nicely, the truck slowed and passed through a set of gates. There was a sign nailed onto the gate.

Frankie peered at it. The letters made no sense, but he liked what he saw under them. It was a picture showing a boy feeding a lamb with a baby bottle! Frankie had seen Ma Halley feed some of the new lambs on the farm that way in the spring. Maybe this was a farm!

He poked his nose over the side board, sniffing. Yup. He smelled animals. He could recognize rabbits, ducks, chickens, sheep, and goats. No one could mistake the smell of goats. But there were so many other smells mixed in — people smells, car smells. Where was he?

He quickly jumped back from the side and tunnelled deeper into the thick grass as the truck stopped. He tried to make himself invisible as he heard a woman call out. Soon there was the quiet murmuring of two voices. In a moment he heard the familiar sound of a pitchfork at work.

Frankie trembled, pressing himself

tightly up against the cab of the truck. The whoosh of the fork grew closer. After a few minutes he saw the gleam of the pitchfork push through the green veil of grass in front of him. He held his breath. On the next swipe, the shiny, sharp tines slashed up in front of his nose. He couldn't control himself and gave a high, sharp scream.

The pitchfork stopped. "Now what have we here?" a voice asked. The grass in front of Frankie was gently parted.

He closed his eyes and his legs buckled under him. He was found. It was all over.

Hands pulled his front legs and slid him along the floor. His eyes were still closed, but he could smell what was in front of him. A person with a faint, pleasant, animal smell.

"Hello there, fellow. How did you get here?" He opened his eyes and peeked up. He saw a woman with a long, yellow braid that hung over one shoulder. She had a tired, friendly face, and she wore a worn shirt and a pair of faded overalls.

"Are you hurt?" she asked, her hands patting all over his body. The skin on her hands was hard, but her touch was gentle. "Hmmm. A few deep scratches and a bad cut on one elbow seem to be all that's wrong with you. And a hungry tummy, probably."

Frankie looked up at her gratefully. He thought about trying to smile, but instead shut his eyes again. He let his forehead rest against the soft shirt.

"Where could he have come from, Lily?" the woman said.

"I don't know what he was doing in the back of the truck, Brenna. Ernie loaded it for me last night. Maybe he got in then. Sure looks like he needs a home, though."

"You think I should keep him?"

"What better place for him, Brenna? You don't have any pigs, do you?"

"No. The kids would really love this guy."

Frankie sighed as the strong fingers scratched behind his ears.

"What do you think, piggy? Would you like to earn your keep here with us?"

Frankie opened his eyes and looked up again. He could almost hear the slow, warm beat of the woman's heart beneath his ear.

"It's a petting farm, pig. All you have to do is let children pat you and admire you. It's not a hard job at all.

And you'll have a cozy bed with some friendly sheep and chickens, and the food trough is always full. What do you say? Will you take the job?"

Frankie's grin was so big it hurt his ears.